Lexile:

LSU ☑yes
SJB ☐yes
BL: 1.7
Pts: 0.5

Dear Parents:

Congratulations! Your child is taking the first steps on an exciting journey. The destination? Independent reading!

STEP INTO READING® will help your child get there. The program offers five steps to reading success. Each step includes fun stories and colorful art or photographs. In addition to original fiction and books with favorite characters, there are Step into Reading Non-Fiction Readers, Phonics Readers and Boxed Sets, Sticker Readers, and Comic Readers—a complete literacy program with something to interest every child.

Learning to Read, Step by Step!

Ready to Read   **Preschool–Kindergarten**
• big type and easy words • rhyme and rhythm • picture clues
For children who know the alphabet and are eager to begin reading.

Reading with Help   **Preschool–Grade 1**
• basic vocabulary • short sentences • simple stories
For children who recognize familiar words and sound out new words with help.

Reading on Your Own   **Grades 1–3**
• engaging characters • easy-to-follow plots • popular topics
For children who are ready to read on their own.

Reading Paragraphs   **Grades 2–3**
• challenging vocabulary • short paragraphs • exciting stories
For newly independent readers who read simple sentences with confidence.

Ready for Chapters   **Grades 2–4**
• chapters • longer paragraphs • full-color art
For children who want to take the plunge into chapter books but still like colorful pictures.

STEP INTO READING® is designed to give every child a successful reading experience. The grade levels are only guides; children will progress through the steps at their own speed, developing confidence in their reading.

Remember, a lifetime love of reading starts with a single step!

Visit us on the Web!
StepIntoReading.com
randomhousekids.com

Educators and librarians, for a variety of teaching tools, visit us at RHTeachersLibrarians.com

ISBN 978-0-399-55888-7 (trade) — ISBN 978-0-399-55889-4 (lib. bdg.)

Printed in the United States of America   10 9 8 7 6 5 4 3 2 1

nickelodeon

BLAZE LOVES TO RACE!

by Mary Tillworth
illustrated by Kevin Kobasic

Random House 🏠 New York

Vroom! Vroom!
The Monster Machines
love to race!

Engines rumble.

The countdown begins.

Three. Two. One.

Go!

Sneaky Crusher
zooms ahead.
He pushes a race ramp
to the side.
Now the ramp
faces the wrong way!

Stripes loves to jump.

He jumps off the ramp.

Whoa!

He lands on a ledge.

Stripes is stuck!

Blaze changes

into a fire truck.

He raises his ladder.

Stripes climbs down.

Blaze and Stripes

speed off.

Rocks block the road.

Zeg can get through!

He loves

to smash and bash.

More rocks fall.

The rocks

bury Zeg.

Zeg is trapped!

Blaze changes
into a bulldozer.

He scoops up the rocks.

Stripes helps.

Blaze and Stripes

clear the way.

Zeg is free!

Starla loves
to twirl her lasso.
Yee-haw!

Oops!

Starla lassoes

a Grizzly Truck.

It pulls her

into the woods!

Blaze, Stripes, and Zeg
make a big
Monster Machine wall.
The Grizzly Truck stops!

Starla pulls

her lasso free.

The friends hurry back

to the race.

Darington loves stunts.
He races through
a loop-the-loop.

Darington loses
his balance.
Oh, no!
He falls!

Blaze and his friends
spread a net.
They hold it high.

Darington lands
in the net.
The friends cheer.
Darington is safe!

Blaze and his friends
zoom to the finish line.

They cross together.

Everyone is a winner!

Blaze loves to race.

But he loves

his friends even more!